Emu's HALLOWEEN

ANNE MANGAN

ILLUSTRATED BY
DAVID CORNISH

Angus&Robertson
An imprint of HarperCollins*Children's*Books

Angus&Robertson

An imprint of HarperCollins*Children'sBooks*, Australia

First published in Australia in 2015
by HarperCollins*Publishers* Australia Pty Limited
ABN 36 009 913 517
harpercollins.com.au

HarperCollins*Publishers*
Level 13, 201 Elizabeth Street, Sydney NSW 2000, Australia
Unit D1, 63 Apollo Drive, Rosedale, Auckland 0632, New Zealand
A 53, Sector 57, Noida, UP, India
1 London Bridge Street, London, SE1 9GF, United Kingdom
2 Bloor Street East, 20th floor, Toronto, Ontario M4W 1A8, Canada
195 Broadway, New York NY 10007, USA

National Library of Australia Cataloguing-in-Publication data:

Mangan, Anne, author.
Emu's Halloween / written by Anne Mangan; illustrated by David Cornish.
978 0 7322 9890 6 (hbk.)
For primary school age.
Emus — Juvenile fiction.
Halloween — Juvenile fiction.
Children's stories — Pictorial works.
Other creators/contributors: Cornish, D.M. (David M), 1972– illustrator.
A823.3

The illustrations in the book were created using pencil and Photoshop, and
coloured using scanned paper and cloth textures
Cover and internal design by Astred Hicks
Colour reproduction by Graphic Print Group, Adelaide
Printed and bound in China by RR Donnelley

6 5 4 3 2 1   15 16 17 18

To my brother, Patrick Mangan, and my publisher, Lisa Berryman,
for their never-ending support and advice, and for making all this possible — AM

To Clare, for her calm and steady wisdom — DC

Emu was having a party, because it was Halloween.
'I want it to be,' said Emu, 'the scariest anyone's seen.'

But Emu had a problem
and said with some dismay,

'I just can't make it scary.
I've been trying to all day!'

As luck would have it, Emu was heard by Cockatoo,
who flew to all the animals to see what they could do.

The animals were excited and rushed to Emu's place.
They could not wait to see the look on Emu's face.

Kangaroo, dressed as a zombie,
was not a pretty sight.

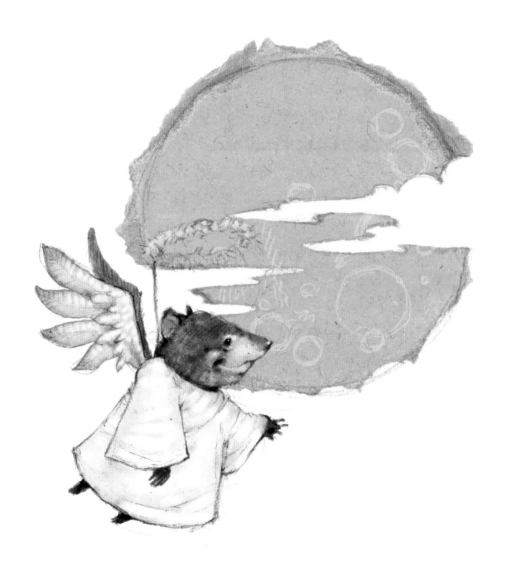

Tassie Devil was an angel,
and felt so good in white.

Koala was Frankenstein's monster,
her fur all in a mess.

Red-back Spider was herself,
which of course was a success.

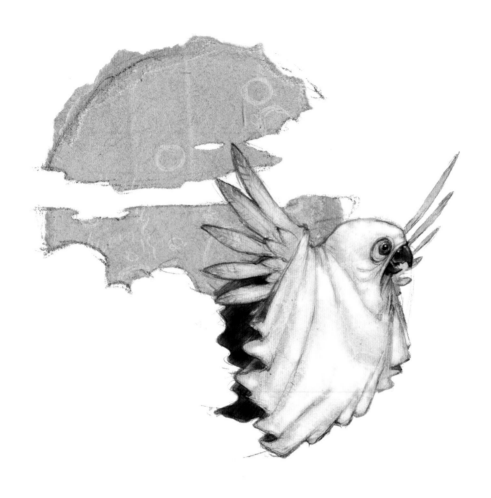

Cockatoo came as a ghost
and floated through the air.

Dressed as Dracula, Echidna
gave himself quite a scare.

When Emu opened up her door, she first got quite a fright!
Then, realising who they were, she screamed out in delight.

The animals wasted no time
deciding what had to be done.

Making Halloween scary
was going to be great fun!

They carved jack-o'-lanterns, cut out paper ghosts
and bats,

made skeletons from sticks,
and painted pictures
of black cats.

Red-back Spider put
up fake webs and said,
'They look so real!

I hope they catch some
insects so that I can have
a meal.'

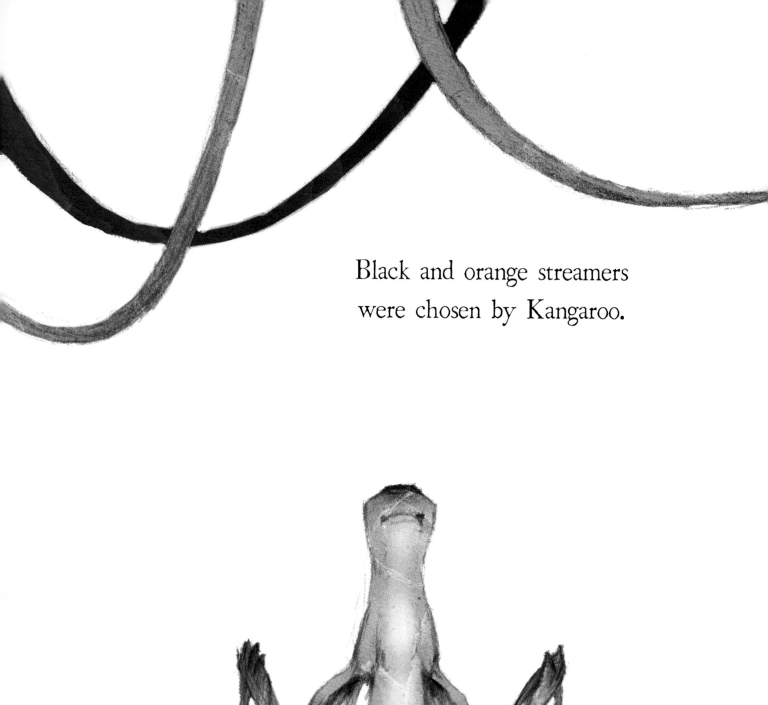

Black and orange streamers
were chosen by Kangaroo.

Tassie Devil mixed up cordials
to make a witches' brew.

Koala spied a ghost gum and
disguised it with a sheet.

'Seeing all those leaves,' she said,
'makes me want to eat.'

So Cockatoo mixed lots of dips,
filled with plastic flies;

made spooky spider cakes,
sand*witches* and pumpkin pies.

Echidna blew up black
balloons and only a few
were popped.

It was then that Emu yelled,
'IT'S HALLOWEEN! It's time we stopped.'

Emu told some scary stories that
frightened everyone.

Getting wet bobbing
for apples, the fruit bat
proudly won.

With blindfolds on they pinned a wart upon a witch's nose,
played pass-the-pumpkin and searched around for buried goblin toes.

They quickly gobbled up all the scary food left to eat
and Emu gave them all some sweets, just like trick-or-treat.

Then, putting a pumpkin on her
head, Emu suddenly yelled out,
'BOO!

It's been the scariest party ever,
thanks to all of ...

YOU!’